ASTERIX AND THE BIG FIGHT

TEXT BY GOSCINNY

DRAWINGS BY UDERZO

TRANSLATED BY ANTHEA BELL AND DEREK HOCKRIDGE

HODDER DARGAUD
LONDON SYDNEY AUCKLAND

Asterix and the Big Fight

ISBN 0 340 04238 9 (cased)
ISBN 0 340 19167 8 (paperbound)

First published in Great Britain 1971 (cased)
Fifteenth impression 1984

First published in Great Britain 1974 (paperbound)
Sixteenth impression 1985

Published by Hodder Dargaud Ltd,
Mill Road, Dunton Green, Sevenoaks, Kent TN13 2YJ

Printed in Belgium by Henri Proost et Cie, Turnhout.

The year is 50 BC. Gaul is entirely occupied by the Romans. Well, not entirely... One small village of indomitable Gauls still holds out against the invaders. And life is not easy for the Roman legionaries who garrison the fortified camps of Totorum, Aquarium, Laudanum and Compendium...

a few of the Gauls

Asterix, the hero of these adventures. A shrewd, cunning little warrior; all perilous missions are immediately entrusted to him. Asterix gets his superhuman strength from the magic potion brewed by the druid Getafix...

Obelix, Asterix's inseparable friend. A menhir delivery-man by trade; addicted to wild boar. Obelix is always ready to drop everything and go off on a new adventure with Asterix – so long as there's wild boar to eat, and plenty of fighting.

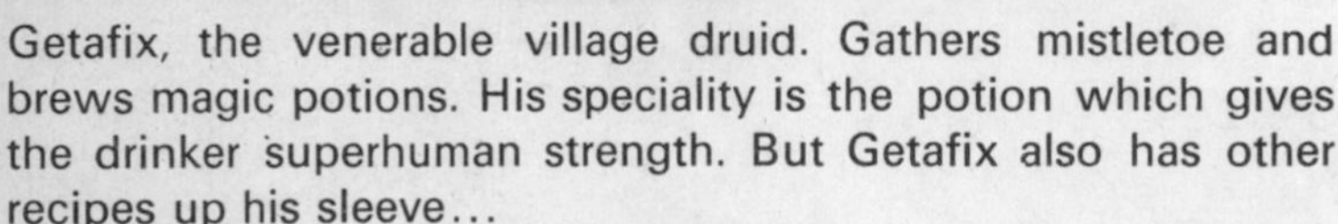

Getafix, the venerable village druid. Gathers mistletoe and brews magic potions. His speciality is the potion which gives the drinker superhuman strength. But Getafix also has other recipes up his sleeve...

Cacofonix, the bard. Opinion is divided as to his musical gifts. Cacofonix thinks he's a genius. Everyone else thinks he's unspeakable. But so long as he doesn't speak, let alone sing, everybody likes him...

Finally, Vitalstatistix, the chief of the tribe. Majestic, brave and hot-tempered, the old warrior is respected by his men and feared by his enemies. Vitalstatistix himself has only one fear; he is afraid the sky may fall on his head tomorrow. But as he always says, 'Tomorrow never comes.'

AT THE TIME OF THE ROMAN OCCUPATION OF GAUL, THERE WERE TWO KINDS OF GAULS...
?

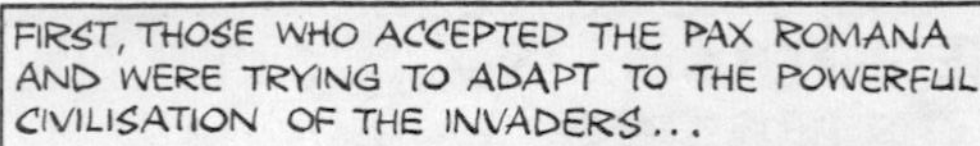

FIRST, THOSE WHO ACCEPTED THE PAX ROMANA AND WERE TRYING TO ADAPT TO THE POWERFUL CIVILISATION OF THE INVADERS...

WHAT ARE THESE PILLARS FOR?
THEY MAKE THE HOUSE LOOK GALLO-ROMAN

IF YOU ASK ME, IT LOOKS MORE GALLO-GREEK...

WHAT A GALL!
HE'S ALWAYS BEEN THAT WAY... IT'S VERY GALLING!

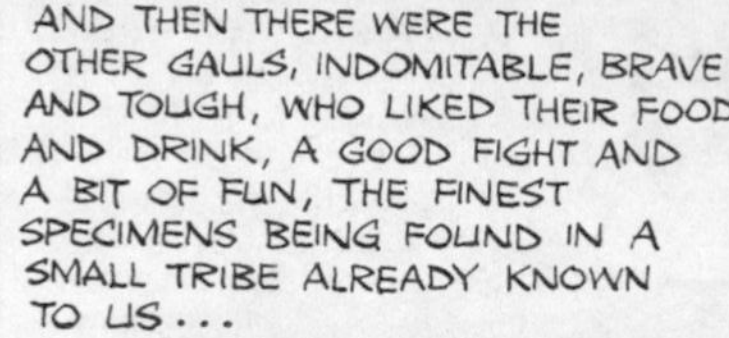

AND THEN THERE WERE THE OTHER GAULS, INDOMITABLE, BRAVE AND TOUGH, WHO LIKED THEIR FOOD AND DRINK, A GOOD FIGHT AND A BIT OF FUN, THE FINEST SPECIMENS BEING FOUND IN A SMALL TRIBE ALREADY KNOWN TO US...

HEY, HERE ARE ASTERIX AND OBELIX BACK FROM HUNTING!

WELL, BOYS, ANY NEWS?
NO. WE GOT A BOAR EACH
BUT I HAD DOGMATIX TO HELP ME. HE'S A GREAT BOARHOUND!!!

OH YES, I FORGOT... WE MET A ROMAN PATROL

THESE ROMANS ARE CRAZY!

MEANWHILE, IN THE FORTIFIED ROMAN CAMP OF TOTORUM...
THE...THE PATROL'S BACK, O CENTURION NEBULUS NIMBUS

BY JUPITER!!! WHAT HAPPENED TO YOU?

ER... WE MET A COUPLE OF GAULS...
AND THEY DID HAVE A DOG WITH THEM...
AND TWO BOARS!
SO THAT MADE FIVE!

THESE GAULS KEEP ON MAKING FOOLS OF US!
WE HAVE TO FIND A SOLUTION, O NEBULUS NIMBUS... IF THEY GET TO HEAR OF THIS IN ROME, YOU'LL BE UNDER A CLOUD!

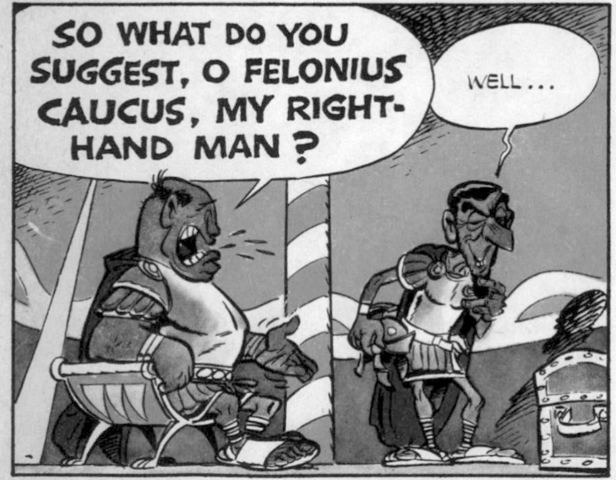
SO WHAT DO YOU SUGGEST, O FELONIUS CAUCUS, MY RIGHT-HAND MAN?
WELL...

I'VE BEEN STATIONED IN THIS COUNTRY A LONG TIME. I KNOW THE GAULISH CUSTOMS. AND THERE'S ONE CUSTOM THAT MIGHT COME IN VERY USEFUL... IT'S CALLED THE BIG FIGHT

THE BIG FIGHT?
YES... WHEN THE CHIEF OF A GAULISH TRIBE WANTS TO BECOME THE CHIEF OF TWO GAULISH TRIBES, HE CHALLENGES ANOTHER CHIEF TO SINGLE COMBAT. THE LOSER AND HIS WHOLE TRIBE SUBMIT TO THE WINNER...

...IF BOTH CHIEFS ARE EQUALLY STRONG, THEY HAVE THE RIGHT TO THROW BALES OF STRAW AT EACH OTHER. THUS THE RESULT IS SAID TO BE DECIDED BY A STRAW VOTE... IF WE HAD A CHIEF WHO SUPPORTED US IN COMMAND OF THOSE INDOMITABLE GAULS, THERE'D BE NO PROBLEM...
BONK!
BIFF!

ALL RIGHT, BUT WHAT CHIEF WOULD BE CRAZY ENOUGH TO CHALLENGE THE TERRIBLE VITALSTA-TISTIX? HIS DRUID'S MAGIC POTION MAKES HIM INVINCIBLE!
I KNOW JUST THE MAN. HE'S A COLLABORATOR, AND AS COLOSSAL AS THE COLOSSEUM!

BY MINERVA! LET'S GO AND SEE THIS CHIEF OF YOURS RIGHT AWAY!
HE LIVES IN THE VILLAGE OF LINOLEUM, AND HIS NAME IS CASSIUS CERAMIX

AND WHILE THE ROMANS SET OFF, LITTERALLY CARRIED AWAY...

IN THE VILLAGE OF LINOLEUM...
CASSIUS CERAMIX
BY JUPITER AND TOUTATIS! I TOLD YOU BEFORE I WANTED SHORT BACK AND SIDES AND TOGAS! WE'RE GALLO-ROMANS!
BUT IT MAKES ME FEEL COLD ALL OVER, CHIEF!

RIGHT! FOR A START, WE'RE GOING TO BUILD AN AQUEDUCT!
AN AQUEDUCT?

BUT, CHIEF CASSIUS CERAMIX, WE DON'T NEED AN AQUEDUCT... THE RIVER FLOWS RIGHT THROUGH OUR VILLAGE AND OUR FIELDS...

THEN WE'LL DIVERT THE COURSE OF THE RIVER! AQUEDUCTS ARE MORE ROMAN!

AND THAT'S ABOUT ENOUGH ARGUING!
PAF!

WHAT DID I TELL YOU?
BY JUPITER! IF ALL THE GAULS WERE LIKE THAT, WE'D BE ROMANO-GAULS!
FLOC!

O CASSIUS CERAMIX!
?

AVE CAESAR! WELCOME TO OUR BELOVED INVADERS!

TERRIBLY SORRY TO INVADE YOU LIKE THIS, BUT CENTURION NEBULUS NIMBUS AND I WOULD LIKE A TALK WITH YOU

THIS IS MY HOUSE... I MEAN MY DOMUS. WON'T YOU COME IN, PLEASE?
DELIGHTED, I'M SURE

ROME SWEET ROME
YOU KNOW THE CUSTOM OF THE BIG FIGHT... WE'D LIKE YOU TO FIGHT ANOTHER CHIEF AND TAKE OVER HIS TRIBE WHEN YOU'VE BEATEN HIM
NOTHING EASIER! WHO IS THIS UNFORTUNATE CHIEF? IT'LL BE SHEER MURDER!

VITALSTATISTIX

VITAL... VITALSTATISTIX!?! BUT IT'LL BE SHEER MURDER!

NO ONE WOULD DREAM OF CHALLENGING VITALSTATISTIX! HE GETS HIS SUPERHUMAN STRENGTH FROM THE MAGIC POTION BREWED BY THE DRUID GETAFIX!
ALL RIGHT, ALL RIGHT ...LET'S CHANGE THE SUBJECT!
NO, DON'T LET'S CHANGE THE SUBJECT!

SINCE THE PROBLEM IS THE DRUID'S POTION, LET'S DISPOSE OF THE DRUID! NO MORE DRUID, NO MORE POTION. NO MORE POTION, NO MORE PROBLEM!

NEXT DAY...
WHERE ARE YOU GOING, O DRUID GETAFIX?
I'M RIGHT OUT OF MAGIC POTION, ASTERIX. I'M OFF TO THE FOREST TO PICK MORE INGREDIENTS

I FEEL WORRIED EVERY TIME OUR DRUID GOES OFF TO THE FOREST ON HIS OWN... BUT HE DOESN'T LIKE COMPANY...

I THINK I'LL FOLLOW HIM AT A DISTANCE...
WHERE ARE YOU GOING, ASTERIX?

I'M GOING TO FOLLOW OUR DRUID. THE FOREST'S NOT SAFE JUST NOW; THE ROMANS SEEM A BIT JUMPY...
THESE ROMANS ARE CRAZY... I'LL COME WITH YOU. I CAN TAKE THIS MENHIR ROUND LATER. IT'S NOT EXPRESS DELIVERY

YOU COULD HAVE LEFT YOUR MENHIR IN THE VILLAGE
WHAT, AND HAVE SOME KID PINCH IT?

IN THE CAMP OF TOTORUM...
THE CAMOUFLAGED DETACHMENT IS READY TO RECEIVE YOUR ORDERS, O NEBULUS NIMBUS
COMING!

EXCELLENT, BY MARS AND JUNO! NOW WHO DARES SAY THE ART OF CAMOUFLAGE IS DYING OUT IN THE ROMAN ARMY?!
ER... NEBULUS NIMBUS...

THAT'S THE GARDEN HEDGE... THE CAMOUFLAGED DETACHMENT...

... IS OVER THERE!

HMM. RIGHT! WHO'S IN COMMAND OF THIS DETACHMENT?
THIS IS OUR BUDDING COMMANDER

RIGHT! GIVE HIM HIS ORDERS!
CAPTURE THE DRUID, DEAD OR ALIVE! PATROL THE FOREST UNTIL YOU FIND HIM. HE OFTEN GOES TO LOOK FOR HERBS THERE. IF YOU SUCCEED, YOU GET A BONUS. IF NOT YOU'LL FIND YOURSELVES IN JUG

ER...CENTURION... IF WE GET A CHOICE, I'D AS SOON FIND MYSELF IN JUG STRAIGHT AWAY...

YOU 'ORRIBLE MAN! RUN LIKE A HARE, AND YOU'D BETTER COME BACK VICTORIOUS, BY MARS!

THAT DIDN'T WORK!
NO, THE HARE DIDN'T GET JUGGED

TRY TO LOOK AS BOTANICAL AS POSSIBLE...
THE BIG SAP...WE'RE TOO BIG TO PLAY COPSE AND ROBBERS!
IF YOU ASK ME, WE'RE ALL SUCKERS!
I'M TREMBLING LIKE A LEAF!
WE'RE NOT OUT OF THE WOOD YET!
I'D AS LIEF NOT BE HERE EITHER, OLD BEAN!
STOP MAKING HORRIBLE JOKES ...WE'VE GOT ENOUGH WORRIES ALREADY!

A LITTLE LATER...

WHERE ARE THEY? WHERE ARE THEY?

WELL, YOU SAID... SO WE DECIDED TO PLANT OURSELVES HERE AND...
ONE MORE TRICK LIKE THAT, YOU WEEDS, AND YOU'LL BE TURFED OUT OF THE ARMY!

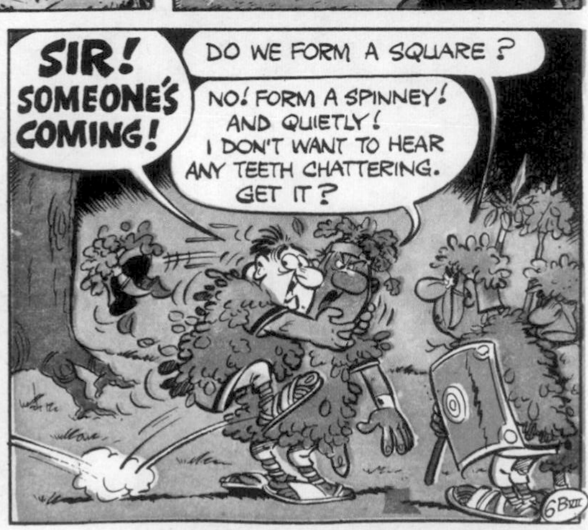
SIR! SOMEONE'S COMING!
DO WE FORM A SQUARE?
NO! FORM A SPINNEY! AND QUIETLY! I DON'T WANT TO HEAR ANY TEETH CHATTERING. GET IT?

LALALALA...
TCHIC!

I'M SURE TO FIND FOUR-LEAVED CLOVERS IN THAT SPINNEY...

FANCY THAT! NOT A FOUR-LEAVED CLOVER, A FIVE-TOED FOOT!

A FOOT?

THERE HE IS! GET HIM! QUICK!

OUR DRUID, SURROUNDED BY ROMANS! WE MUST RESCUE HIM!

I'LL GET RID OF THEM FOR YOU!
NO, OBELIX! NOOOOO!

BOOOM!

BRAVO, OBELIX! OH, VERY WELL DONE!
WELL, I DID GET RID OF THOSE ROMANS, DIDN'T I?
POF! POF! POF!

HERE COMES THE PATROL!
AHA!

MISSION ACCOMPLISHED. WE GOT THE DRUID!

WITH A PILUM?
ER... NO... WITH A MENHIR...

... AND WE LEFT HIM UNDER THE MENHIR. NO HUMAN BEING COULD SURVIVE A BLOW LIKE THAT!

I HOPE YOU'RE RIGHT... BUT I SOMETIMES WONDER IF THOSE GAULS ARE HUMAN... ANYWAY, WE'LL LET CASSIUS CERAMIX KNOW HE CAN COME AND CHALLENGE VITALSTATISTIX!

MEANWHILE.
ALL THE SAME, A LITTLE TAP WITH A MENHIR COULDN'T HAVE DONE HIM ANY HARM... MAYBE HE ATE SOMETHING HEAVY FOR LUNCH...
WE'RE COMING TO THE VILLAGE... I'M GOING TO TRY AND REVIVE HIM!

JUST A LITTLE TAP ON THE HEAD WITH A MENHIR... NOTHING TO SPEAK OF...

DONE IT! HE'S COMING BACK TO HIS SENSES! HE'S VERY STRONG, OUR DRUID, ESPECIALLY IN THE HEAD

HOW ARE YOU FEELING?

VERY WELL, THANK YOU... AND WHO MIGHT YOU BE, MY DEAR SIR?

I'M ASTERIX! YOU KNOW ME... ASTERIX!
PLEASED TO MEET YOU

HAHAHA! WHAT A FUNNY LITTLE CHAP YOU ARE!
?

I'M GLAD TO SEE YOU SO WELL. I ALWAYS KNEW A LITTLE MENHIR COULDN'T...

HOHOHO! YOU REALLY ARE FUNNY, FATTY! HEEHEEHEE!
FATTY? WHAT FATTY?

OH DEAR, OH DEAR! TEEHEE HEE HEE!
NOW THEN, GETAFIX! DON'T YOU RECOGNIZE ME, OLD FRIEND?

TAP! TAP! TAP!

HAHAHAHA! HOHOHO!
HE REALLY HAS LOST HIS MEMORY!
AND HIS MIND! HE SEES FAT MEN WHEN THERE AREN'T ANY!
WHAT EXACTLY IS GOING ON?
THE DRUID DOESN'T RECOGNIZE ANYONE!

LET ME PLAY HIM A TUNE... HE'LL RECOGNIZE MY GENIUS
WE COULD TRY... IT'S RATHER VIOLENT TREATMENT, BUT SOMETIMES A SHOCK...

IF YOU WERE THE ONLY GAUL IN THE WORLD...
CLONG! CLING!
HAHA! HOHO!

WHAT'S HE LAUGHING FOR?
HEEHEEHEE! DON'T STOP, MY DEAR SIR, IT'S VERY NICE! ENCORE! ENCORE!
HE'S CRAZY!
HE'S CRAZY!
TOLD YOU SO!
HE'S CRAZY!
HE'S CRAZY!
HE'S CRAZY!
HE'S CRAZY!
BOF! BOF! BOF!

HA!HA!HA!
HO!HO!HO!
YOU TAKE THE DRUID BACK TO HIS HUT, OBELIX. I'M GOING TO TALK TO OUR CHIEF
AS I HAVE BEEN ASKED FOR AN ENCORE...

THAT WILL DO!!

HOW ARE WE GOING TO CURE HIM, ASTERIX?
TO THINK HOW EASILY HE COULD HAVE MADE POTIONS TO CURE HIMSELF LIKE A SHOT...

THE POTION! THE MAGIC POTION THAT GIVES US SUPERHUMAN STRENGTH!
PLAC!

LET'S HOPE HE CAN REMEMBER THE FORMULA! IF NOT, THOSE ROMANS ARE GOING TO GET THE BETTER OF US! THEY OUTNUMBER US A HUNDRED TO ONE, AND THEY'RE BETTER EQUIPPED TOO!

O GETAFIX, CAN YOU REMEMBER THE FORMULA OF THE MAGIC POTION?
MAGIC POTION?

WHAT MAGIC POTION? YOU MUST LET ME HAVE A LOOK AT THIS MY DEAR SIR... IT SOUNDS INTERESTING

WE MUST WARN THE WHOLE VILLAGE. THIS IS SERIOUS!
YOU KNOW... THE POTION! I FELL INTO IT WHEN I WAS A BABY!
HO!HO!HO! I CAN SEE I'M REALLY GOING TO ENJOY MYSELF HERE... IT'S ALL SO QUAINT AND FUNNY... YIPPEEE!
10

FRIENDS, GAULS, COUNTRYMEN! I HAVE A SERIOUS ANNOUNCEMENT TO MAKE! OUR DRUID HAS LOST HIS MEMORY AND CAN NO LONGER MAKE THE MAGIC POTION, THE SECRET OF OUR STRENGTH... OUR STOCKS OF POTION ARE EXHAUSTED, SO NOW WE ARE VULNERABLE. WE MUST KEEP THIS DISASTER SECRET, AND HOPE NO ONE CHALLENGES US BEFORE OUR BELOVED DRUID IS CURED!
CLING!
PAF!

IN ANY CASE, NEVER FORGET THAT WE HAVE NOTHING TO FEAR EXCEPT THE SKY FALLING ON OUR HEADS!

BUT THE SKIES ARE LOWERING... A ROMAN MESSENGER ARRIVES AT THE VILLAGE OF LINOLEUM...
WHERE DO I FIND YOUR CHIEF CASSIUS CERAMIX?
HE'S INSPECTING PROFESSOR BERLIX'S SCHOOL OF MODERN LANGUAGES AT THE MOMENT
11A
MENSA, MENSA, MENSAM, MENSAE, MENSAE, MENSA...
SCHOOL

AVE!
COLISEUM ROMANUS
A B C

COME ON! COPY LITTLE PRAWNSINASPIX WHO SALUTED OUR ROMAN FRIEND SO NICELY!

I HAVE AN IMPORTANT MESSAGE FOR YOU FROM CENTURION NEBULUS NIMBUS, O CASSIUS CERAMIX!
RIGHT, LET'S LEAVE THE ROOM

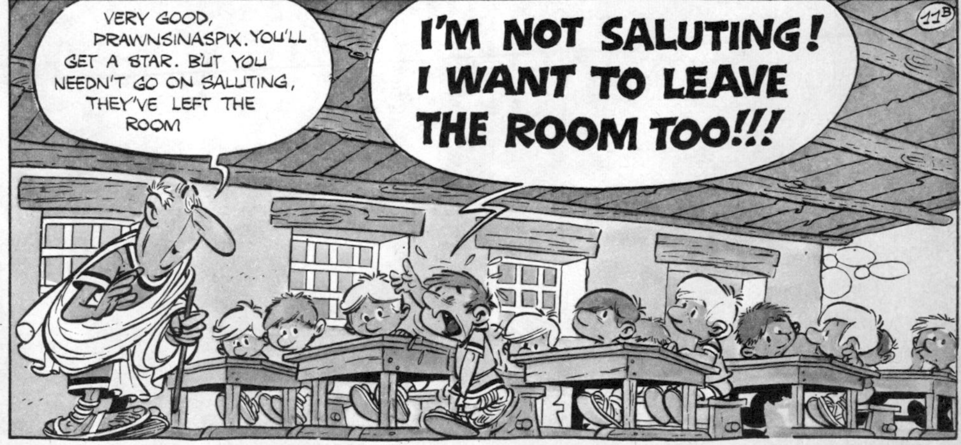
VERY GOOD, PRAWNSINASPIX. YOU'LL GET A STAR. BUT YOU NEEDN'T GO ON SALUTING, THEY'VE LEFT THE ROOM
I'M NOT SALUTING! I WANT TO LEAVE THE ROOM TOO!!!
11B

I'VE COME TO TELL YOU THE DRUID GETAFIX HAS BEEN DISPOSED OF. YOU CAN CHALLENGE CHIEF VITALSTATISTIX
YOU'RE... YOU'RE QUITE SURE THE DRUID'S GONE?

QUITE SURE! WE DEFEATED HIM! IT WAS A FAMOUS VICTORY!
WELL THEN, TELL YOUR CENTURION I'LL CHALLENGE MY RIVAL TOMORROW!

I'M GOING TO BEAT VITALSTATISTIX! I'M THE GREATEST! AND THEN, WITH THE HELP OF THE ROMANS, I SHALL BEAT ALL THE OTHER CHIEFS AND I'LL BE THE ONLY CHIEF LEFT IN GAUL!

I WILL MAKE GAUL A NEW ROME! I'LL BUILD ROMAN BATHS. I'LL COMMAND THE GAULS TO WASH ALL OVER EVERY DAY, IN STRICT ROTATION. IT WILL BE CALLED THE ORDER OF THE BATH!

BACK IN THE GAULISH VILLAGE, OUR FRIENDS' LONG VIGIL IS DRAWING TO A CLOSE...
HMMMMMHEEHEE! HEEHEEHEE HMMM!
ANYWAY, IT GOT HIM INTO A GOOD MOOD...
A TINY LITTLE MENHIR LIKE THAT... IT ONLY TICKLED HIM!
OBELIX, MY FRIEND, YOU'RE BEGINNING TO GET ON MENHIR... ON MY NERVES!
12A

WHAT'S THAT?
SOUNDS LIKE CACOFONIX SINGING
I'LL GO AND SEE
BAHAAAHOOO

BOOAAAAAHOOOOOOOO
?

I HAVE COME TO ANNOUNCE THE ARRIVAL OF MY CHIEF CASSIUS CERAMIX. HE WANTS TO TALK TO YOUR CHIEF VITALSTATISTIX. AVE!

12B
HM... CERAMIX... I DON'T MUCH LIKE THE SOUND OF THIS. HE'S A BRUTAL, AMBITIOUS, UNSCRUPULOUS RENEGADE
ASTERIX, TELL HIM TO STOP LAUGHING WHENEVER HE LOOKS AT ME!

CERAMIX IS COMING, CHIEF!
COME ON, HURRY UP! THEY'RE CALLING ME!
IF YOU WILL KEEP FIDGETING...

GET DOWN! THEY'RE COMING!
THERE YOU ARE!

BAAAAHOOOOOUUUUUUU
BAAAAAOOOUUUUUUUUUUUHHH!
WHAT A ROW!
IT HAS A CERTAIN SOMETHING...
13A

AVE!
WOTCHER!

THIS IS A SUMMIT CONFERENCE!
YOU'RE TELLING US!

I HAVE COME TO THROW DOWN THE GAUNTLET! I AM CHALLENGING YOU TO SINGLE COMBAT!
?!!

A CHALLENGE!
A CHALLENGE!

YES, BUT...
ACCORDING TO OUR LAWS, THE WINNER WILL BECOME CHIEF OF THE LOSER'S TRIBE! THE FIGHT WILL TAKE PLACE NEXT CALENDS!
13B

LISTEN, CERAMIX...
NOT ANOTHER WORD! VICTURUS TE SALUTO! I TURN MY BACK ON YOU!
TCHIP!

CLUCK!

?!

ME! NOT YOU! IF WE ALL TURN OUR BACKS I GET BACK WHERE I STARTED!

WHAT'S GOING ON HERE? WHAT ARE THOSE TWO DOING UP THERE?
14A

HEY, THAT'S...
THAT'S OUR DRUID GETAFIX!

ABOUT TURN! AND FAST!
US OR YOU?

THIS IS NO TIME TO BE CLEVER! IF I COME DOWN THERE YOU'D BETTER WATCH OUT!

WOOOAHAHA HEEHEEHEE!
THIS IS A NICE MESS! THAT BRUTE'S AS STRONG AS ME, OUR DRUID'S IN NO STATE TO MAKE THE MAGIC POTION - AND THE FUTURE OF THE TRIBE DEPENDS ON THE RESULT OF THIS FIGHT!

LET'S HOPE OUR DRUID WILL SOON BE FEELING BETTER!
HOHOHO HOHOHAHA HEE HEE HEE HEE
14B

IN THE FORTIFIED CAMP OF TOTORUM...
YOU TOLD ME GETAFIX THE DRUID HAD BEEN DISPOSED OF! NOT ONLY HAS HE NOT BEEN DISPOSED OF, HE'S IN A VERY GOOD MOOD! HE CAN'T STOP LAUGHING!

I'VE CHALLENGED VITALSTATISTIX, AND NOW I CAN'T WITHDRAW WITHOUT SUBMITTING TO HIM. I'M NOT SURE I WON'T, RATHER THAN GET MYSELF MURDERED...

THANKS VERY MUCH FOR YOUR ADVICE, FELONIUS CAUCUS! SO NOW I LOOK LIKE HAVING TWO REBEL VILLAGES ON MY HANDS INSTEAD OF ONE! OH, WON'T CAESAR BE PLEASED!

DON'T LET'S GET UPSET. WE STILL HAVE PLENTY OF TIME TO SEND PATROLS OUT TO THE FOREST TO CAPTURE THE DRUID...
15A

QUOD ERAT DEMONSTRANDUM
OH, QUITE EASILY DONE!

MEANWHILE, IN THE GAULISH VILLAGE...
GETAFIX, YOU MUST LISTEN TO ME! YOU HAVE TO PREPARE THE MAGIC POTION TO GIVE OUR CHIEF SUPERHUMAN STRENGTH!
LOOK, WHO IS THIS GETAFIX YOU KEEP ON ABOUT?

LET'S GET EVERYTHING READY. PERHAPS HIS MEMORY WILL COME BACK. OBELIX, YOU GO AND FETCH THE INGREDIENTS FROM GETAFIX'S HUT, AND A CAULDRON

WOOAHAHAHA!
THAT FAT MAN IS PRICELESS!
ASTERIX, IF YOU DON'T TELL HIM TO STOP, DRUID OR NO DRUID, I SHALL TAKE THIS CAULDRON AND I'LL...
YOU'VE ALREADY DONE THAT WITH A MENHIR, OBELIX!
15B

AND WHAT DO I DO NOW?
WELL, YOU PUT THE INGREDIENTS IN THE CAULDRON... THEN YOU MAKE THE POTION

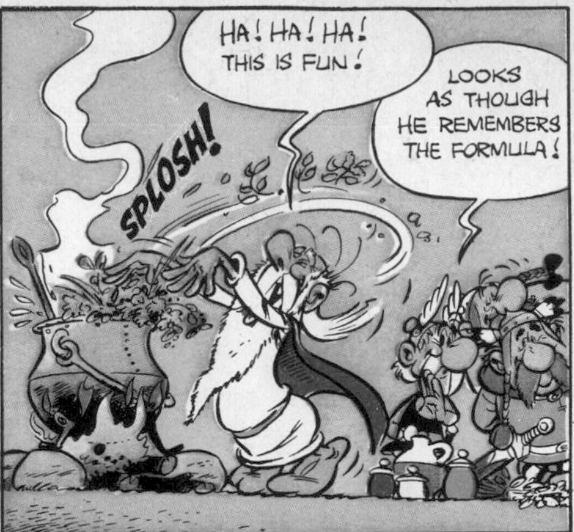
HA! HA! HA! THIS IS FUN!
SPLOSH!
LOOKS AS THOUGH HE REMEMBERS THE FORMULA!

DO I PUT THIS IN TOO?
BLOP! BLOP! BLOP!
ER... IF YOU LIKE...

BOOOM!

HA!HA!HA THIS IS A NICE GAME! COME ON! LET'S START AGAIN!
?!
OBELIX, GO AND FIND ANOTHER CAULDRON!

SOON AFTERWARDS...
TERRIBLY SORRY, GENTLEMEN, NOTHING'S HAPPENING THIS TIME... IT'S A DUD
BLOP! BLOP! BLOP!
MAYBE HE'S DONE IT. LET'S GO AND SEE

BLOP! BLOP! BLOP!

BOOOM!

TEEHEEHEE! IT WORKED! IT WORKED!
?!
I WONDER IF WE'RE GOING TO GET ANYWHERE THIS WAY?
WE'LL JUST HAVE TO TAKE POT LUCK!
16

COMMANDED BY LEGIONARY INFIRMOF-PURPUS, A PATROL VENTURES INTO THE FOREST...
THIS IS ODD... WHERE ARE THE GAULS? ONE OF THEM OUGHT TO HAVE KNOCKED US OVER THE HEAD BY NOW!

BOOOM!
HEAR THAT?
WHAT ARE THEY UP TO? WHAT ON EARTH ARE THEY UP TO?
CLAC! CLAC! CLAC! CLAC!

LOOK! A CAULDRON!
WHERE?

CLONCK

BACK TO THE CAMP! QUICK!

THEY'RE MAKING HORRIBLE NOISES IN THAT VILLAGE, AND FIRING CAULDRONS GREAT DISTANCES, VERY HARD...
CAULDRONS? HOW DARE THEY TAKE POT SHOTS AT MY LEGIONARIES?!

WHAT'S MORE, THIS ONE'S BEEN USED TO MAKE FISH SOUP!
SNIFF! SNIFF!
OH, SO THAT'S THE WAY IT IS? RIGHT, WINKLE THAT IDIOT OUT OF THERE AND TELL HIM HE'S VOL-UNTEERED TO GO AND SPY ON THE GAULS!

THIS IS A PRETTY KETTLE OF FISH!
SPLATCH!

IN THE GAULISH VILLAGE...
THAT ONE DIDN'T GO OFF BANG!
IF IT DIDN'T GO OFF BANG, PERHAPS HE'S DONE IT?
LET'S HAVE A LOOK...
BLOUP! BLOUP!

SOMEONE OUGHT TO TASTE IT TO FIND OUT IF IT IS THE MAGIC POTION...
YES, BUT IF IT ISN'T IT MIGHT BE INDIGESTIBLE...
I WILL TASTE IT... AFTER ALL, THE DRUID MAY BE OFF COLOUR BECAUSE OF MY MENHIR!
BLUP! BLUP! BLUP!
TEE HEE HEE, TEE HEE HEE!

NO, OBELIX! I AM THE CHIEF. IT'S MY JOB TO TASTE IT!
BUT IF YOU GO OFF BANG, CERAMIX WILL BECOME OUR CHIEF, AND HE WON'T EVEN HAVE TO FIGHT FOR IT!

WE REALLY WANT A ROMAN TO TASTE IT... WE'RE SURE TO FIND A ROMAN SOMEWHERE TO DO THIS LITTLE JOB FOR US!

MEANWHILE IN THE FORTIFIED CAMP OF TOTORUM...
HAS INFIRMOFPURPUS GONE YET?
NO. HE WON'T COME OUT OF HIS CAULDRON
18A

ARE YOU GOING TO COME OUT OF THERE?
NO!

AREN'T YOU ASHAMED OF YOURSELF, HIDING IN A CAULDRON SMELLING OF FISH!
NO, I AM NOT ASHAMED OF MYSELF, HIDING IN A CAULDRON SMELLING OF FISH!

I'D RATHER BE HERE INSIDE A CAULDRON SMELLING OF FISH THAN IN THE GAULISH VILLAGE OUTSIDE A CAULDRON SMELLING OF FISH!

I'LL POACH YOU ALIVE IN YOUR CAULDRON SMELLING OF FISH!
ALL RIGHT. NOT TOO MUCH SALT, PLEASE
18B

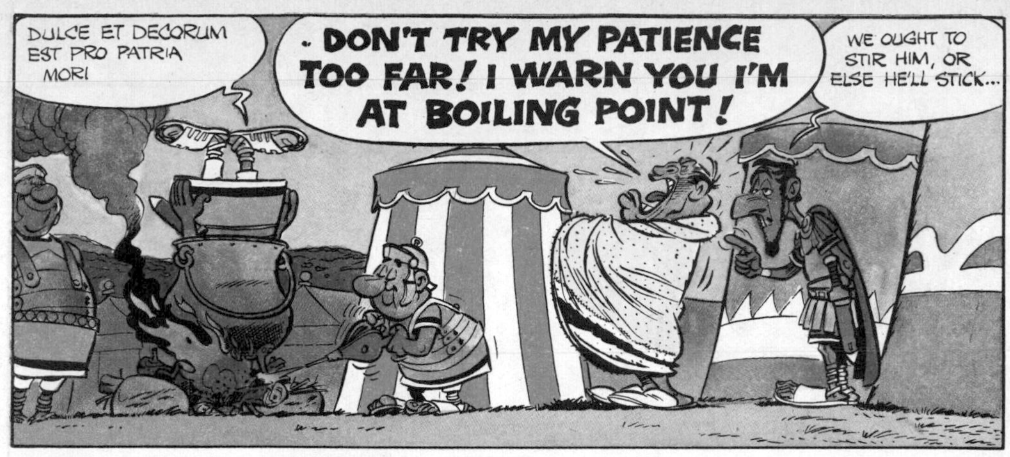
DULCE ET DECORUM EST PRO PATRIA MORI
- DON'T TRY MY PATIENCE TOO FAR! I WARN YOU I'M AT BOILING POINT!
WE OUGHT TO STIR HIM, OR ELSE HE'LL STICK...

NOW, ARE YOU COMING OUT OR AREN'T YOU?
I... I'M NOT QUITE READY YET...

ALL RIGHT THEN, JUST TO KEEP BODY AND SOLE TOGETHER... BUT IT'S UNDER PROTEST... WHY THE FLAMING HURRY?

I CONGRATULATE YOU ON YOUR UNSOLICITED HEROISM! NOW YOU ARE GOING TO SPY ON THE GAULS... YOU'LL BE IN NO DANGER, WELL CAMOUFLAGED!

SOON AFTERWARDS...
LOOK! HERE COMES INFIRMOFPURPUS!
HE LOOKS A BIT SOUR!
19A

AND HE SMELLS OF FISH!
IT MUST BE A CRAB APPLE TREE!

HOHOHOHO HAHAHA!
IDIOTS!

THE GALLANT LEGIONARY REACHES THE FOREST...
I'M NEAR ENOUGH THE GAULISH VILLAGE NOW... I'LL JUST PLANT MYSELF HERE...

TO-WHIT, TO-WHOO!
?

GET OUT, YOU BEASTLY BIRD. YOU'LL DRAW ATTENTION TO ME. SHOO, YOU TWIT!
TO-WHIT?

SHOO! YOU SHOO!
TO-WHOO! TO-WHOO! A TALKING TREE! IT SMELLS OF FISH TOO! VERY REMARKABLE! I WILL NEVER LEAVE THIS PLAICE!
19B

WE POSITIVELY MUST HAVE A ROMAN TO TASTE OUR DRUID'S POTION
OH, YOU CAN FIND THEM ANYWHERE IN THE WOODS AT THIS TIME OF YEAR

HELP! THE GAULS! I'LL TRY TO LOOK INCONSPICUOUS!

TO-WHIT, TO-WHOO!

SOMEONE'S CALLING TO US!
TO WHO?

TO-WHIT, TO-WHOO!
OVER THERE! LET'S HAVE A LOOK!

IT'S AN OWL! TO-WHIT, TO-WHOO!
TO-WHIT, TO-WHOO!
HELP!

YOU CAN'T EAT IT, BUT IT'S AMUSING. I THINK I'LL TAKE IT HOME TO DOGMATIX. THEN HE'LL HAVE A LITTLE FRIEND
WOULDN'T HE GROWL AT AN OWL?

ANYWAY, WE'RE NOT HERE FOR FUN... COME ON!
PHEW!

PHEW? DID YOU HEAR SOMEONE SAY PHEW?
PHEW? WHO?
TO-WHOO!

NO! IT WASN'T ME! I NEVER SAID PHEW! IT WAS TO-WHOO! THAT WAS THE OWL. HE SAID TO-WHOO! NOT PHEW!
??

MUMMY!
THIS REALLY IS A MOST ENTERTAINING TREE... AN ENTIRELY NEW VARIETY!

POMPEY'S BODY LIES A-MOULDERING IN THE GRAVE..
... BUT HIS SOLE GOES MARCHING ON..
WOODMAN, WOODMAN SPARE THAT TREE!
WOOF!

THIS IS FISHY, TOO!
LET'S HOPE IT'S NOT A RED HERRING!

DON'T HURT ME! I'M A WARRIOR LIKE YOU, EVEN IF I AM AN ENEMY!... YOU WOULDN'T WANT TO FIGHT AN ENEMY WARRIOR, WOULD YOU?

WE'RE NOT GOING TO HURT YOU, WE'RE OFFERING YOU A SPOT OF SOUP, THAT'S ALL WE'RE GOING TO DO TO YOU
THAT'S ALL YOU'RE GOING TO DO?
THAT'S ALL WE'RE GOING TO DO!
TO-WHIT, TO-WHOO!
BLOP! BLOP! BLOP!
TEEHEEHEEHEE!

GLOUP! GLOUP! GLOUP!

WOOHAHAHA!
HE'S GONE GREEN! HOW DO YOU DO THAT?

WH... WHAT'S HAPPENING TO ME?
NO LUCK YET... WE'LL HAVE TO MAKE ANOTHER POTION...
DON'T WORRY, ROMAN, WE'LL SEE TO IT
FUNNY... HE TURNS GREEN AFTER THEY DIG HIM UP...
TEEHEEHEEHEE HOHOHOHO!

SOON AFTERWARDS...
HOHOHO! I AM HAVING A NICE TIME HERE!

THE UNHAPPY INFIRMOFPURPUS DRINKS SEVERAL HIGHLY-COLOURED POTIONS ONE AFTER ANOTHER...
GLOUP! GLOUP!

... WITH RESULTS THAT...

... WHILE DECORATIVE...

... ARE NOT...

...THE RESULTS...

... DESIRED!

!
THIS MUST BE A VERY HEALTHY DRINK... IT GIVES YOU A GOOD COLOUR
WOOAHAHAHA HAHAHAHA!

STOP IT! I'VE HAD ENOUGH! I WANT MY SCHOOLGIRL COMPLEXION BACK THAT MADE ME SO MANY CONQUESTS ON THE APPIAN WAY!

YIPPEEE!
DON'T BE SO COLOURIC... I MEAN CHOLERIC... IT MAKES YOU GO PURPLE. WE'RE GOING TO HAVE ONE LAST SHOT AND THEN WE'LL LEAVE YOU ALONE
I AM FEELING BLUE!

SOON AFTERWARDS...
LOOK, ASTERIX, HE'S SKY-BLUE...
THAT'S BECAUSE HE'S TURNED PALE... COME ON, DRINK THIS!

22

I'VE GOT MY PINK AND WHITE COMPLEXION BACK!
MAYBE THIS IS THE RIGHT POTION, ASTERIX!
MAYBE...

HOW ARE YOU FEELING, ROMAN?
FINE... IN THE PINK...

POSITIVELY BUOYANT...
!?!

...VERY BUOYANT!
?!?

CATCH ME!
CATCH HIM! HE'S FLYING AWAY!!!

WHAT'S MORE, HE CAN FLY! NOW THAT'S WHAT I CALL A REAL FRIEND!

OOOOOH!
TOWHOOOOO!
SHALL I BRING HIM DOWN? I CAN GET HIM WITH MY MENHIR FROM HERE...
?
NO! HE'S GONE WITH THE WIND!... WELL, THE POTION'S NO GOOD. WE'LL HAVE TO THINK OF SOMETHING ELSE!

THE FORTIFIED ROMAN CAMP OF TOTORUM...

HEY!
?

SEND UP AN ANCHOR... AND NONE OF YOUR CLEVER REMARKS!
?

SOON AFTERWARDS...
WHAT DO YOU WANT, AND WHAT HAVE YOU GOT AT THE END OF THAT ROPE?

COME AND SEE FOR YOURSELF, O CENTURION... YOU'D NEVER BELIEVE IT, BY JUPITER!

?!!

THAT'S NO WAY TO APPEAR BEFORE YOUR COMMANDING OFFICER! COME DOWN HERE AT ONCE!!!
I CAN'T! I'M AS LIGHT AS A FEATHER!

FEATHER-BRAINED, MORE LIKE! GET HIM DOWN!

NOW THEY'VE SHOWN THEIR TRUE COLOURS! I'D SAY THEIR DRUID HAS GONE CRAZY! HE'S FORGOTTEN HOW TO PREPARE THE MAGIC POTION!

WELL, WELL, VERY INTERESTING!
YOU CAN LET HIM GO NOW!

24

ALL IS WELL! THAT MENHIR OBVIOUSLY MADE SOME IMPACT ON THE DRUID! HE HAS LOST HIS POWERS FOR MAKING MAGIC POTION
LET'S GET AT THE GAULS! THERE ARE A LOT MORE OF US THAN THEM!

IT'S QUITE UNNECESSARY TO RISK INJURY... LET CASSIUS CERAMIX DO THE DIRTY WORK FOR US. WE'LL ATTACK ONLY IF HE LOSES

GNNNNEE HEEHEE!
HOHA HAHA!
HEY... WHAT ABOUT ME?

HE FLIES AT NIGHT, JUST LIKE ME! HE'S THE NICEST TREE I EVER LIGHTED UPON!
WHAT'S UP WITH YOU?

WHAT'S TO BECOME OF ME? YOU'RE STARTING TO GET ME DOWN... I HOPE!

DON'T WORRY! THE EFFECTS OF THESE GAULISH POTIONS ARE ONLY TEMPORARY! IT WILL SOON WEAR OFF. HAVE A GOOD NIGHT!

SURE ENOUGH, IN THE MIDDLE OF THE NIGHT...
BAOOM!

HM... THE POTION'S WORN OFF

WHILE THE ROMANS ARE DEAD TO THE WORLD, THE GAULS PASS A SLEEPLESS NIGHT...
WE NEED ANOTHER DRUID TO CURE OUR DRUID!
WHAT A GOOD IDEA, BY TOUTATIS!
ZZZZ

I KNOW A DRUID LIVING NEAR HERE. HIS SPECIALITY IS CURING THE MENTALLY DISTURBED. HE'S CALLED PSYCHOANALYTIX
25

WE'RE GOING TO FETCH PSYCHOANALYTIX!
CLUCK!

WE HAVEN'T COME ACROSS ANY ROMAN PATROLS. THAT SPY MUST HAVE SAID WE'D RUN OUT OF MAGIC POTION, SO THERE'S NO NEED TO WATCH US
THERE'S NO FUN IN TRAVELLING THESE DAYS, THE ROADS ARE SO SAFE

AFTER AN UNEVENTFUL JOURNEY...
PSYCHO-ANALYTIX DRUID
HERE WE ARE

WE'D LIKE TO SEE THE DRUID!
DO YOU HAVE AN APPOINTMENT? IF NOT, YOU'LL HAVE TO WAIT
26 A

PEOPLE COME FROM ALL OVER THE PLACE TO BE TREATED BY THE DRUID...
WAITING GLADE
CONSULTING HUT

THAT'S A SHY BARBARIAN. IT'S A GREAT DRAWBACK IN HIS LINE
Not in the way, am I?

THIS ONE'S AFRAID THE SKY MAY FALL ON HIS HEAD

THIS ONE THINKS HE'S A WILD BOAR!
GRROUINKK! GRRROUINNK!
OBELIX!
SNIFF! SNIFF!

NO ONE KNOWS WHO THIS ONE THINKS HE IS
?
26 B

HUT
NEXT, PLEASE, MISS BICARBONÁT-OFSODA!

HUT
GRRROINNNKK! GROUINNNNN!

SOON AFTERWARDS...

NEXT!
DOESN'T HE THINK HE'S A WILD BOAR ANY MORE?
WELL, HE DOES, A BIT, BUT THE DRUID HAS TAUGHT HIM TO BEG, SO IT DOESN'T SHOW SO MUCH
GROUINNNK!

HUT

SOON AFTERWARDS...
I'M CURED! I'M CURED! I'M NOT FRIGHTENED OF THE SKY FALLING ON MY HEAD ANY MORE!

THIS DRUID'S AMAZING. I'M SURE HE'LL CURE GETAFIX
IT'S YOUR TURN

COME IN! COME IN!

LIE DOWN, PLEASE
WHO, ME?
?!
27

NOW THEN, WHAT SEEMS TO BE THE TROUBLE ?... DON'T TELL ME, I KNOW...
?!
?!

YOU'VE GOT THE IDEA YOU'RE FAT, AND THAT IS MAKING YOU ILL. YOU'RE WRONG. THERE'S NO NEED TO FEEL ILL BECAUSE YOU'RE TOO FAT...

BUT I'M NOT ILL !!!
NO, O DRUID, HE'S NOT ILL...

GOOD HEAVENS ! IF I WAS AS FAT AS THAT IT WOULD MAKE ME ILL
WE CAME TO FETCH YOU TO CURE GETAFIX. HE'S THE ONE WHO'S ILL

GETAFIX ? DEAR OLD GETAFIX, WHO TAUGHT US EVERYTHING WE KNOW ? GETAFIX, WHO HAS SECRETS KNOWN ONLY TO HIMSELF? WHAT ARE WE WAITING FOR ?
28A

BICARBONATOFSODA, I'M GOING AWAY FOR A FEW DAYS ... PASS ME THE CAULDRON OVER THERE...

HUT
?!? WHAT'S BEEN GOING ON HERE ?
IT'S THAT BARBARIAN YOU CURED OF SHYNESS. HE SAID HE WANTED TO CATCH UP WITH HIS WORK

SOON AFTERWARDS...
BOOHOOHOOO!
??

BOOHOOHOOHOO!
I'M TOO FAT!
I'M TOO FAAAAT!
28B

NONSENSE, OBELIX, YOU'RE NOT TOO FAT AT ALL...
YOU'RE ONLY SAYING THAT TO CHEER ME UP!
BOOHOOHOO!
TAP! TAP! TAP!

SNIFF! SNIFF!
DING! DONG! DONG! DING!
YOU MUST BRING HIM TO SEE ME... I'LL CURE HIM FOR YOU

SOON AFTERWARDS...
AH, HERE YOU ARE AT LAST! COME ALONG, I'LL TAKE YOU TO GETAFIX!
WOOF!

GETAFIX, MY DEAR OLD FRIEND!
?
POC!

WOOHAHAHAHOHOHO!
WHO'S THIS LITTLE SHRIMP?

HOHO! HEEHEE!
THAT'S IT, A SHRIMP! HE'S A REAL LITTLE SHRIMP!
?

I'D RATHER BE BUILT ON GENEROUS LINES THAN A LITTLE SHRIMP, WOULDN'T YOU, ASTERIX?
OF COURSE, OBELIX, NATURALLY... LET THE DRUID GET ON WITH HIS WORK...
POF! POF! POF! POF!

RIGHT! NOW I'VE CURED THE FAT ONE, I CAN HAVE A LOOK AT GETAFIX

HEEHEE! HOHO!
TELL THAT ELEPHANT TO SHUT UP, OR I SHALL GO ALL TO POT!
SCROTCH! SCROTCH!

OBELIX, YOU MUST HAVE A MENHIR TO DELIVER! DON'T KEEP YOUR CUSTOMERS WAITING!
HUH! I'D RATHER BE AN ELEPHANT THAN A SHRIMP...

ESPECIALLY A POTTED SHRIMP!
29

PUT MY CAULDRON ON TO BOIL... IT LOOKS AS THOUGH I'LL HAVE TO MAKE SOME POTIONS

SOON AFTERWARDS...
I KNOW SOME VERY CLEVER TRICKS WITH A CAULDRON TOO!
BUMP!
NOW REMEMBER, WHATEVER YOU DO DON'T CONTRADICT THE PATIENT

WHAT HAPPENED TO HIM? SOME SORT OF A SHOCK?
YES, IT WAS A MENHIR GOT HIM DOWN

I DON'T THINK IT WAS THAT AT ALL. YOU ALWAYS MAKE OUT IT WAS MY FAULT. YOU'RE NOT GOING TO TELL ME THAT A LITTLE TAP WITH A...

OBELIX! DON'T BE SO PIG-HEADED. IT DOESN'T TAKE A DRUID TO KNOW THAT IT WAS ALL ON ACCOUNT OF YOUR MENHIR!

EXCUSE ME, BUT IT DOES TAKE A DRUID TO BE ABLE TO JUDGE THESE THINGS... HOW EXACTLY DID HE GET THIS TAP WITH A MENHIR?

LIKE THAT...
BONG!
OBELIX!

OBELIX, GO AND DELIVER YOUR MENHIR AND LEAVE US ALONE!!!
WELL, HE DID ASK...

IF YOU'RE GOING TO BE LIKE THAT, I SHAN'T HELP YOU ANY MORE. SORT IT OUT BY YOURSELVES!

HE'S COMING TO!
HOW ARE YOU, O DRUID?
I BEG YOUR PARDON, MY DEAR SIR?
30

HE DOESN'T REMEMBER A THING!
HE'S IN THE SAME STATE AS GETAFIX!

LOOK, MY DEAR SIR, I CAN PREPARE SOME VERY INTERESTING CONCOCTIONS!
LET ME HAVE A GO TOO!

THERE'S ONLY ONE THING FOR IT, O VITALSTATISTIX... YOU MUST GET INTO TRAINING FOR YOUR FIGHT WITH CERAMIX!
QUITE RIGHT. I DON'T THINK WE CAN RELY ON THE DRUIDS
JUST TRY THIS, MY DEAR SIR!

WHAT A PITY OBELIX ISN'T CHIEF INSTEAD OF ME!
HEE HEE HEE HEE!
YOUR TURN NOW, MY DEAR SIR!

HE FELL INTO A CAULDRON OF POTION WHEN HE WAS A BABY, AND IT HAD A PERMANENT EFFECT ON HIM...
HOHOHOHO!

IT'S AGAINST THE LAW TO ABDICATE IN FAVOUR OF HIM... SO THAT'S NO GOOD
HAHAHAHA!

ASTERIX, I APPOINT YOU MY TRAINER FOR THE BIG FIGHT!
HEEHEEHEE! HOHOHO! HAHAHA

OUR FIRST SESSION WILL BE TOMORROW AT THE CRACK OF DAWN. YOUR DIET... RED MEAT, NO MORE BEER, NOTHING BUT GOAT'S MILK

WHAT A LOVELY BLUE!
WHAT A LOVELY RED!
37

DAWN HAS NOT YET CRACKED WHEN...
ZZZ! ZZZ!

?

ON YOUR FEET, CHIEF! WE'LL START YOUR TRAINING WITH A BIT OF RUNNING!
COMING, ASTERIX!

COCKADOODLEDOO!

ONE, TWO, ONE, TWO! COME ON, BOYS, PUT SOME BEEF INTO IT, BY TOUTATIS!
?

NO, NO... THAT'S NOT THE WAY, VITALSTATISTIX! LET ME SHOW YOU!

THAT'S BETTER
MUCH BETTER
VERY MUCH BETTER
HM! HE'S NOT BEEFING SO MUCH NOW!
NOW YOU MUST HAVE SOME FIGHT TRAINING. YOU NEED A SPARRING PARTNER...
PUFF! PUFF! PUFF!

I CAN DO THAT JOB...
I'M NOT SURE WHETHER...
HE'S RIGHT. OBELIX IS IDEAL FOR THE PART. I SHAN'T BE AFRAID OF HURTING HIM

VERY WELL, LET'S STAR...
TCHONK!

BRAVO! OH, VERY CLEVER, OBELIX! WHEN YOU'RE AROUND THERE'S NO NEED FOR ANY ROMANS IN GAUL!!!
I WAS ONLY TRYING TO HELP...
VIII 32

O, CHIEF VITALSTATISTIX, YOU HAVEN'T LOST YOUR MEMORY, I HOPE?
NOT ONLY HAVE I NOT LOST MY MEMORY, I'M IN NO DANGER OF FORGETTING THAT PUNCH EITHER!

WHILE VITALSTATISTIX GOES ON WITH HIS TRAINING, IN THE VILLAGE OF LINOLEUM HIS REDOUBTABLE OPPONENT CASSIUS CERAMIX IS TRAINING JUST AS HARD...
NEXT!
POF!
POF!
POF!

TCHOK!

NEXT!
I WISH THIS FIGHT WAS OVER!
THIS TRAINING IS GETTING ON TOP OF ME!
HE'S CERTAINLY PILING IT ON!

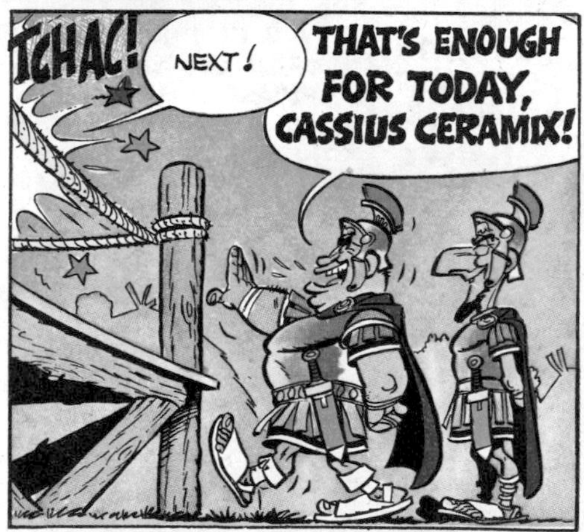
TCHAC!
NEXT!
THAT'S ENOUGH FOR TODAY, CASSIUS CERAMIX!

YOU JUST CAN'T LOSE! WITH-OUT ANY MAGIC POTION, YOUR OPPONENT WILL NEVER BE ABLE TO STAND UP TO YOU!

AND NEITHER WILL THE OTHER GAULISH CHIEFS! I SHALL CHALLENGE THEM ONE BY ONE AND BECOME CHIEF OF ALL GAUL!
BONG!

(SOTTO VOCE) HMM... THIS GAUL IS A BIT TOO AMBITIOUS. HE COULD BECOME DANGEROUS
(SOTTO VOCE) I'VE BEEN THINKING ABOUT THAT. AFTER HE'S WON, WE'LL SEND HIM ON A LITTLE TRIP TO ROME... IN CHAINS. HE'LL FIND OTHER SPARRING PARTNERS IN THE CIRCUS ARENA

YOU SOMETIMES ARE QUITE BRIGHT, FELONIUS CAUCUS!
PAF!

A BIT TOO BRIGHT! AFTER CASSIUS CERAMIX HAS WON, YOU'LL GO WITH HIM TO ROME AND BE HIS SPARRING PARTNER IN THE CIRCUS!

WHILE THE COMBATANTS ARE IN TRAINING, THE ROMANS BUILD THE RING FOR THE BIG FIGHT OUTSIDE THE CAMP...

AND AS THE FIGHT AROUSES A GREAT DEAL OF PUBLIC INTEREST, NOMADIC BARBARIANS PUT UP THEIR SIDESHOWS NEARBY...
LIQUORIX BOARS

1 SESTERTIUS
DODGEM CHARIOTS
1S

SHOOTING RANGE
5 BULL'S-EYES WINS A JAR OF BULL'S-EYES
CATAPULTS: 1 BRONZE COIN A SHOT
SPEARS: 2 BRONZE COINS A THROW

SWITCHBAX
5 BRONZE COINS

THE GREAT DAY DAWNS AT LAST, AND A VAST CROWD ASSEMBLES, THEIR SHOUTS AND LAUGHTER MINGLING WITH THE SMELL OF BOAR AND CHIPS...
A GOLD COIN FOR ANYONE GOING ONE ROUND WITH THE MIRMILLO!
GET YOUR SOUVENIR MENHIRS HERE!
WILL THE PARENTS OF LITTLE ICELOLLIX PLEASE COME TO COLLECT HIM AT THE LOST CHILDREN'S TENT?
CHILDREN'S COMIX! 3 BRONZE COINS THE SLAB!
A PRESENT FROM THE ARMORICA FUN FAIR
MENAGERIX SEE THE FABULOUS ANIMALS
W.H.Smix
BOUM!
34

GARRISON... SHOULDER ...ARMS! TO THE RINGSIDE... FORWARD ...MARCH!

HEY, INFIRMOFPURPUS, I WONDER IF YOUR OWL WON'T END UP BRINGING US BAD LUCK?
HE'S NOT MY OWL, AND IT'S NOT MY FAULT IF HE KEEPS FOLLOWING ME!
TO-WHIT, TO-WHOO!

CASSIUS CERAMIX ARRIVES AT THE RINGSIDE...

MEANWHILE...
O VITALSTATISTIX, IT'S TIME TO GO!
HEAVE AWAY, BOYS!

FRIENDS! I PROMISE TO DO MY UTMOST TO WIN, BY TOUTATIS!
LONG LIVE THE CHIEF!

I ONLY WANTED TO GIVE THEM A LITTLE SONG OF ENCOURAGEMENT...

OUR FRIENDS' VILLAGE IS ALMOST DESERTED... ONLY THE TWO DRUIDS ARE LEFT...
JUST TASTE THAT, MY DEAR SIR. I THINK YOU'LL BE AMUSED BY ITS PRESUMPTION!
I'VE MIXED A LITTLE SOMETHING MYSELF WHICH I THINK WILL SURPRISE YOU

... WITH OBELIX, A QUARRY TO REMORSE
OBELIX QUARRY

LONG LIVE VITALSTATISTIX! BRAVO! VITALSTATISTIX, BY BELENOS!
CASSIUS CERAMIX FOR EVER! CASSIUS CERAMIX, BY JUPITER!

THIS FIGHT WILL GO ON UNTIL ONE OF THEM THROWS IN THE TOWEL! THE STAKES ARE AS FOLLOWS: THE WINNER RECEIVES THE HOMAGE OF VITAL... OF THE LOSER AND HIS TRIBE!

ON MY RIGHT, THE GALLO-ROMAN CHIEF CASSIUS CERAMIX!
THE GREATEST!

ON MY LEFT, THE GAULISH CHIEF VITALSTATISTIX!
INDOMITABLEST!

THIS IS AN ALL-IN CONTEST. TO YOUR CORNERS, AND WHEN YOU HEAR THE BUCINA, COME OUT FIGHTING! AND MAY CASSIUS CER... MAY THE BEST MAN WIN! ALEA JACTA EST!

WHERE'S OBELIX?
AT HOME. HE'S SAD BECAUSE HE THINKS ALL THIS IS HIS FAULT

GO AND GET HIM! WE'LL NEED HIM IF THINGS TURN NASTY AFTER THE FIGHT!

AND SO THE BIG FIGHT BEGINS!
PAAAA
!PR

BACK AT THE VILLAGE, OBELIX IS AT ROCK BOTTOM...
IT'S ALL MY FAULT... WHEN I THINK THAT ONE LITTLE TAP WITH A MENHIR...
ELIX
RRY

A TAP WITH A MENHIR! THEN WHY SHOULDN'T ANOTHER TAP CURE OUR DRUID?

I'M CERTAIN NO ONE ELSE WOULD HAVE THOUGHT OF THIS SOLUTION! YOU'VE GOT TO BE PRETTY INTELLIGENT TO THINK OF A SOLUTION LIKE THAT!
OBELIX QUARRY
?

MEANWHILE...
WHAT SHALL WE DO NOW?
SUPPOSE WE PUT ALL THE REST OF THE INGREDIENTS INTO ONE CAULDRON? WOULDN'T THAT BE FUN!

I BET WE COME OUT IN RED AND GREEN CHECKS!
OR YELLOW WITH BLUE SPOTS! HEEHEEHEEHEE!
SPLASH!
SPLOSH!

PLOP!
PLOP!

YOU HAVEN'T SEEN MY FRIEND? THE FAT ONE?

NO, ASTERIX, I HAVEN'T SEEN OBELIX
EEEEEECH!

ASTERIX! YOU CALLED ME ASTERIX! SO YOU'RE BETTER!

PAFFF!
!!!

OBELIX!... DID YOU THROW THIS MENHIR?
OF COURSE. TO CURE OUR DRUID...

YOU'RE NOT GOING TO TELL ME I'VE DONE THE WRONG THING AGAIN?!
(WITH GREAT RESTRAINT) LISTEN, WE HAVEN'T GOT TIME TO ARGUE...
POF! POF. POF.

STOP ARGUING AND GET ME OUT OF HERE!
!
POTOPONPOTOPON!

TOUTATIS BE PRAISED! OUR DRUID IS STILL CURED!
WHAT D'YOU MEAN, STILL? I'VE JUST CURED HIM WITH MY CAREFUL NURSING!

WHAT EXACTLY HAS BEEN HAPPENING BETWEEN THOSE TWO KNOCKS?
LET ME EXPLAIN, GETAFIX...

AFTER ASTERIX'S STORY...
QUICK! EMPTY THAT CAULDRON! BRING SOME HOT WATER! I'M GOING TO MAKE SOME MAGIC POTION!
I'M AFRAID THE FIGHT HAS ALREADY STARTED, AND IF CASSIUS CERAMIX WINS WE ARE CONDEMNED TO BE HIS SUBJECTS!

HEY, WAIT A BIT! I HAVEN'T HAD ANY OF THAT YET!

NO, OBELIX, I DON'T NEED YOU TO TASTE THE MAGIC POTION! IT WOULD BE MORE USEFUL IF YOU FOUND SOMETHING TO CARRY IT IN

SOON AFTERWARDS...
IT'S NO FUN HERE ANY MORE. I'M OFF!

OUR THREE FRIENDS ARE NEARING THE SPOT WHERE THE BIG FIGHT...
WHY ARE YOU BRINGING THAT MENHIR, OBELIX? I DON'T LIKE TO SEE YOU WITH ONE OF THOSE THINGS ANY MORE!
IT MIGHT COME IN HANDY, ASTERIX, YOU NEVER KNOW!

...HAS BEEN GOING ON FOR HALF AN HOUR...
WILL-YOU-STOP-RUNNING!!!
SWWIFFF

YOU SHARE OUT THE POTION WHILE I GO AND TELL THE CHIEF
PERHAPS I COULD...
NO! YOU FELL IN IT WHEN YOU WERE A BABY!

CHIEF VITALSTATISTIX!
YES? WHAT IS IT?

GETAFIX IS CURED. WE'RE FIGHTING FIT NOW!

AHA! THAT BIT OF NEWS REDOUBLES MY STRENGTH

AH! PUFF! PUFF! AT LAST... PUFF! PUFF! ...YOU'VE STOPPED RUNNING!

TCHAC!
HMMMMFFF!

SPLATCH!

I'M THE MOST BEAUTIFUL! I'M THE GREATEST! I'M THE CHAMPION!

SINCE I AM THE WINNER, I REMAIN CHIEF OF MY OWN TRIBE AND I ALSO TAKE OVER THE TRIBE OF CERAMIX!
ONE MOMENT, GAUL!

WE HAVE OTHER PLANS! VERY WELL, YOU MAY HAVE WON THAT FIGHT! NOW WE'RE GOING TO SEE WHETHER YOUR PEOPLE CAN DEFEAT THE INVINCIBLE ROMAN LEGIONS!

IN... INVINCIBLE ROMAN LEGIONS... ER... IS THAT US?

WE WEREN'T EXPECTING ANYTHING ELSE FROM YOU DOUBLE-DEALING ROMANS! VERY WELL, WE SHALL MEET YOU ON THE PLAIN!

LONG LIVE OUR CHIEF!
LONG LIVE VITALSTATISTIX!

SOON AFTERWARDS...
LEGIONARIES! I AM LEADING YOU TO A VICTORY AS CERTAIN AS IT WILL BE GLORIOUS! FORWARD MARCH!
ER...

O CENTURION, WE DON'T WANT TO BE AWKWARD, BUT EVERY TIME WE ATTACK THESE SAVAGES, THEY START LAUGHING AND THEY MAKE MINCEMEAT OF US...

THEY'LL LAUGH THE OTHER SIDE OF THEIR FACES THIS TIME, LEGIONARIES! THEIR DRUID HAS GONE MAD, THEY HAVE NO MAGIC POTION AND WE OUTNUMBER THEM A HUNDRED TO ONE!
NO MAGIC POTION? A HUNDRED TO ONE?

DOWN WITH THE GAULS, COMRADES, BY JUPITER!!!
FORWARD, BY JUNO!!!
GOOD BOYS!

COMMANDED BY ITS OFFICERS, THE ROMAN LEGION BEGINS TO CARRY OUT ITS IMPRESSIVE MANOEUVRES

MEANWHILE, THE GAULS ARE WAITING...

SUDDENLY...

NOW, BOYS,
FORWARD!

THE GAULISH TACTICS SEEM LESS SKILFUL THAN THOSE OF THE ROMANS...
STOP PUSHING AT THE BACK!
THOSE FOUR ON THE LEFT ARE MINE!
SINCE WHEN, MAY I ASK?
CHARGE FIRST, FIGHT LATER!
HOHO! HEEHEE! HOHO!
THIS IS MORE LIKE IT!

... BUT THEY SEEM STRIKINGLY EFFECTIVE!
I GIVE IN!
WHAT?
HOHO! HEEHEE! HOHO!
THIS IS MORE LIKE IT!
BONG! BONG! BONG!
BANG! BING!
PAF!
GRRRRRR!
TCHRAAC!

OH DEAR, OH DEAR! IT'S TIME TO SLIP AWAY...
I SAID: I GIVE IN!
WHAT?
BONG! BONG! BONG!

BOING!

COMMANDED BY ITS OFFICERS, THE ROMAN LEGION ENGAGES UPON A NEW MANOEUVRE KNOWN AS 'THE HASTY RETREAT'
YOU'LL HEAR MORE ABOUT THIS, FELONIUS CAUCUS! I'LL REMEMBER YOUR GOOD ADVICE!
BING! BANG! BONG!

HALT! THE BATTLE'S OVER!
ALREADY? WE'VE ONLY JUST BEGUN!

AND THERE FOLLOWS THE QUIET AFTERMATH OF BATTLE...
OOOH!
TO-WHOO!
42

ISN'T THAT YOUR MENHIR THERE, OBELIX?
SO IT IS! IT MUST HAVE SLIPPED OUT OF MY HANDS DURING THE BATTLE.
ISN'T THERE SOMEONE UNDERNEATH IT?

?
IT'S CERAMIX!
I BEG YOUR PARDON, MY DEAR SIR?

CERAMIX, THE LAW GIVES ME THE RIGHT TO TAKE COMMAND OF YOUR TRIBE AND TO TREAT YOU AS A VANQUISHED ENEMY... BUT I PREFER TO BE GENEROUS!

I AM LETTING YOU GO FREE WITH YOUR PEOPLE! I ASK ONLY THAT YOU DON'T FORGET THAT YOU ARE A GAUL, AND NEVER SUPPORT THE ROMANS AGAIN. NOW GO!
WHERE TO, MY DEAR SIR?
LONG LIVE VITALSTATISTIX! LONG LIVE GAUL!

LIFE HAS CHANGED IN THE GALLO-ROMAN VILLAGE OF LINOLEUM. THE INHABITANTS HAVE RETURNED TO THEIR TRADITIONAL GAULISH WAYS; THEY LIKE THEIR FOOD AND DRINK, A GOOD FIGHT AND A BIT OF FUN...

... AND OCCASIONALLY THEY ARE NOT ABOVE SENDING THE ROMAN PATROLS PACKING...
YOU SEE, IF YOU WANT THE EMPIRE TO LAST YOU MUST BE ABLE TO LET THINGS DROP WHEN THE OCCASION DEMANDS IT
WAIT FOR US!

AS FOR CERAMIX, HE HAS BECOME THE MOST COURTEOUS CHIEF IN ALL GAUL. HE WAS PROBABLY THE ORIGINATOR OF THE FAMOUS REPUTATION FOR POLITENESS THAT THE FRENCH ENJOYED... ONCE UPON A TIME...
WOTCHER, CHIEF!
GOOD MORNING, MY DEAR SIR!

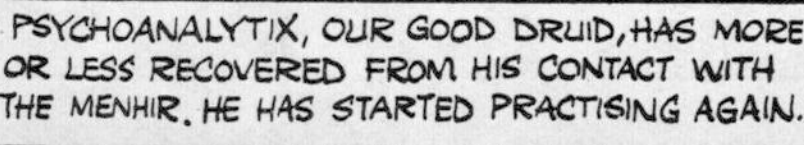
PSYCHOANALYTIX, OUR GOOD DRUID, HAS MORE OR LESS RECOVERED FROM HIS CONTACT WITH THE MENHIR. HE HAS STARTED PRACTISING AGAIN...

HUT

... AND IN ANY EVENT HIS FAME MAKES UP FOR ANY MINOR SIDE EFFECTS
HUT

A BOAR, BY TOUTATIS!

HAHAHA HAHAHAHAHAHAHAHA!

the end

PRINTED IN
proost Turnhout (Belgium)

PRINTED IN BELGIUM